The Story of
ROSIE'S RAT

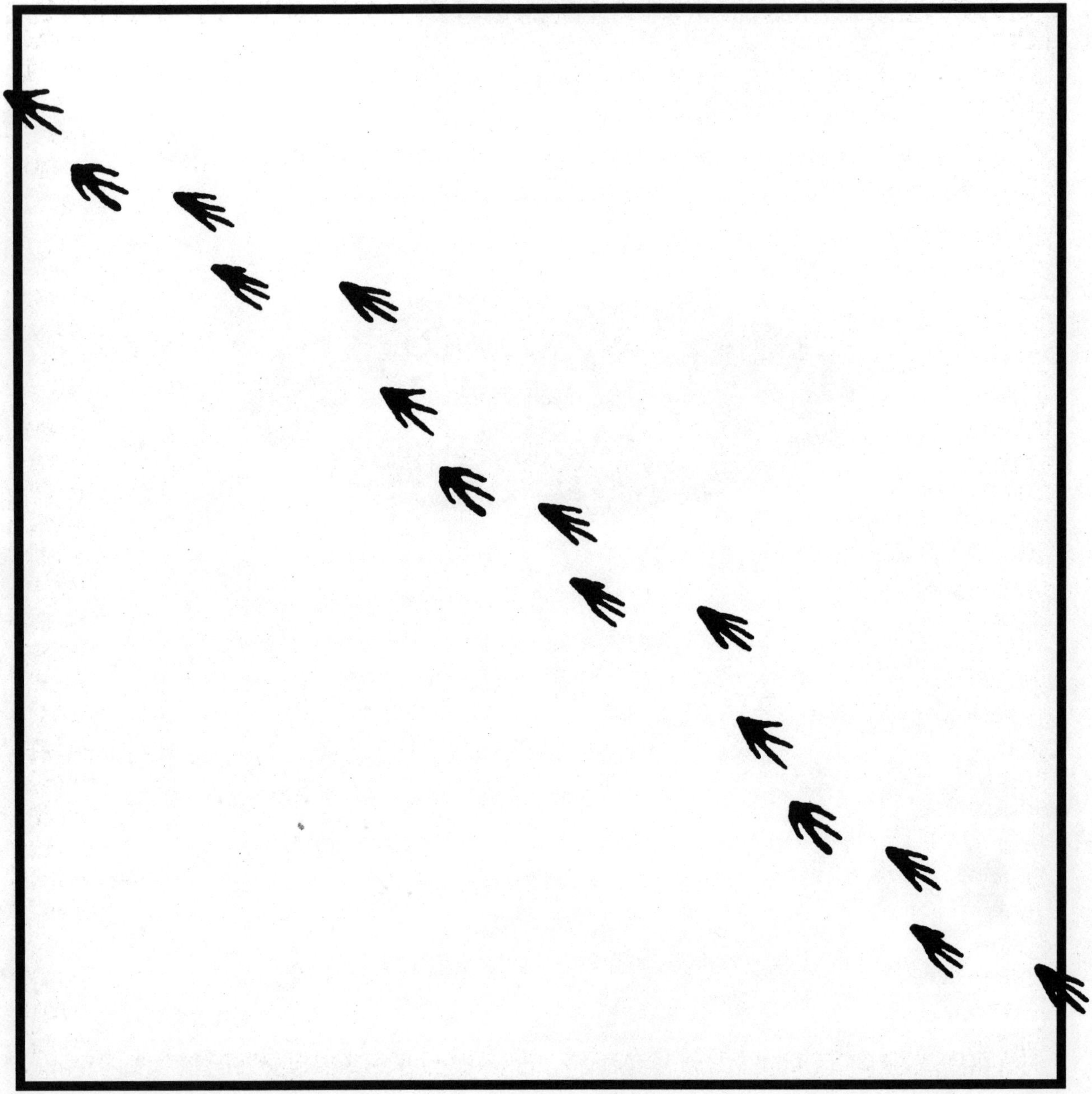

The Story of ROSIE'S RAT

a True Story

told and illustrated by

Porter P. Swentzell
& Rose Swentzell

La Alameda Press • Albuquerque

Originally published in a different version
by *Flowering Tree Institute* —
a permaculture phenomenon
at Santa Clara Pueblo, New Mexico

•

All rights reserved
by the authors and publisher
& if you want to make this into a movie
or a Broadway play
you need to get our permission!

•

© Copyright 1994
Porter P. Swentzell & Rose Swentzell

•

ISBN: 0~9631909~5~4

•

La Alameda Press
9636 Guadalupe Trail NW
Albuquerque, New Mexico
87114

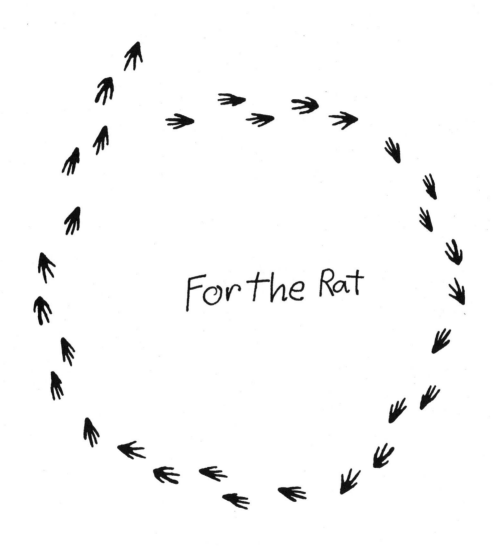

For the Rat

Rosie is a little girl.
She was seven years old
and in the second grade
when this amazing
story took place...

ROSIE: Ida (my teacher) had two rats.
She was giving them away 'cause they would get out
of their cage and run all over the classroom at night.
If you wanted one, you had to sign a paper.
I signed one 'cause I wanted a rat,
'cause they were so cute.

•

We wrote our names on little pieces of paper
and put them in a box.
Then Ida picked out two names.
Two boys got their names picked
and so got the rats.
I didn't get anything.
I felt awful 'cause I did not get anything.

Miryn was too rough and couldn't take care
of his rat, so he killed it.
After that, I came home from school
and I was crying 'cause I didn't get one.
Joel (my stepfather) gave me three dollars
and Ma Ma took me to TG&Y,
and we got a rat.
She's white with red eyes.
She has a long fuzzy tail and I call her Monta.
I love her so much.
We fed her and took care of her.
She lived with us for a long time,
but not a year.

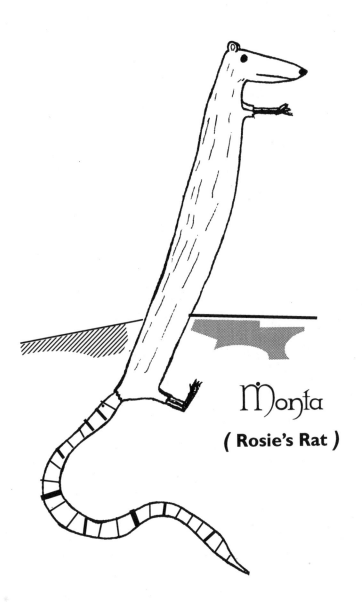

Monta

(Rosie's Rat)

Porter Paul Swentzell

Porter is a big boy.
He was eight years old
when this story happened.
He is Rosie's brother and he likes rats too,
but not as much as the Civil War.

A UNion Soldier

Porter's Rat

Porter: Rosie's Rat was lonely
so we went to the mall and bought
a rat at the pet store.
It was black and white and she was fat.
We took it home and put it with Rosie's Rat.
A few weeks later she had a baby.
but the baby rat died.

We made a cage for them
because they kept getting out of their old cage.
It was tall and had a board sticking out
so they could climb up to it.
Their cage was covered with wire screening.
We fed them dog food.
They were happy for awhile
but then they got anxious to get out.

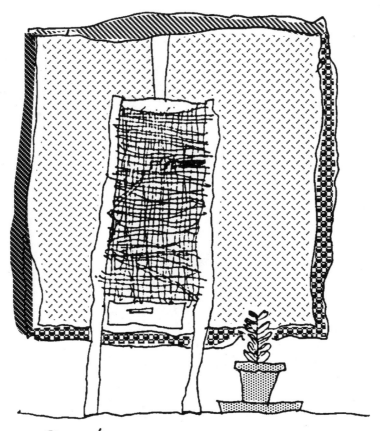

Rat cage

me playing
With rats

ROSIE: It was fun to play with the rats.
They crawl all over you,
up behind your neck, down to your feet.
They would scratch with their claws
when they climbed up you.
They would pick up their food with their hands
and take little bites out of it.
They were soft and clean because
they would clean themselves like a cat.
They ran really fast.
We would let them out of the cage once in awhile
and let them run around.
They would sometimes pull your hair.

These are
baby turkeys

One day we got baby turkeys at the feed store in town.
They were small and they were not like the big turkeys,
they sounded cute. There were ten.
You have to feed them.
You have to put wire over their cage
because they will jump out.
They need to be inside
because they are just babies.
They were next to the rat cage.

PORTER: When the rats got anxious,
they chewed a hole in the wire screening
on their cage and got out,
so Ma Ma put them in the courtyard.
They lived in the courtyard a while.
Rosie's Rat went and lived under the shed.
We put the baby turkeys outside in a cage.

One night, my rat, went through the cage
and killed the baby turkeys
and ate their brains out.

So we buried them...
Only one was still alive.

I felt weird.

ROSIE: I felt sad when they told me
about the turkeys.
I felt sorry for them.
Ma Ma and Joel told Porter
to take my rat and Porter's rat away.
He took them down to a stream.
It was a quarter of a mile away.
A quarter of a mile is less than a mile.

PORTER: First of all, I was playing with my cousin
when Ma Ma called me and I came.
She said that I had to take the rats away.
She put them in a bag.
I started to walk down the road.
On the way there, I was crying
because I was sad that I had to take them away.

I finally got to a good place near the stream,
a quarter of a mile away.
I let them go in-between two trees.
I came back crying.
I got home and cried some more.

ROSIE: I was at school when it happened.
When I got home they told me
they had taken the rats away.
I was so sad because I loved my rat.

•

Three weeks later, Porter saw my rat in the garden.

•

PORTER: I was building paper houses
when I looked out the window
which looked out into the courtyard and I saw Rosie's rat!
I hollered out that Rosie's rat is in the courtyard,
to Ma Ma and Joel.
Ma Ma came running down the stairs.
Joel caught the rat.
She was all hurt up. She was bit on the tail.
She was missing some claws and she was kind of bloody.

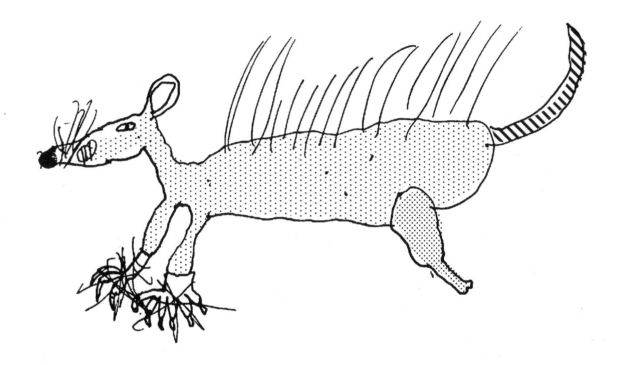

That evening, we were going to a field
down on the other side of the Pueblo.
So we took her with us to the field and left her there.
Ma Ma didn't want her to come back.

ROSIE: The field is on the other side
of the highway and more.
I would go down our driveway, up our driveway,
then I'd take a road going right until I get to the stop sign.
If you put twenty houses together,
that's how long the road is.
Then you go down, just a room long,
then I would take the big highway, go right
and walk a long while.
I would go down to the rehab and go down the road
and then I'd go to my left,
and then I would go on a little road, right—
a short road,
and then it is right in front of me.

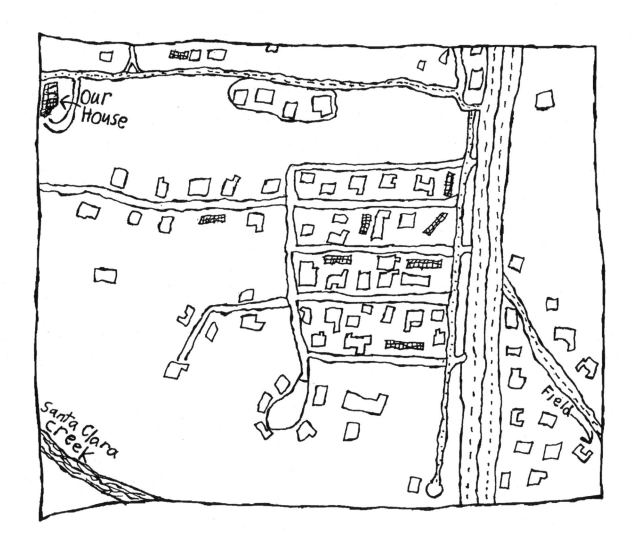

PORTER: We left the rat down in the field.
I just put it down by the fence.
It was grassy and had weird flowers and alfalfa.
The rat looked around and ran around looking at things.
I just put it down and walked away.
She went out of my sight.

We were irrigating our field of corn, beans, chile and melons.
We left the field all muddy and came home.
We left the rat there,

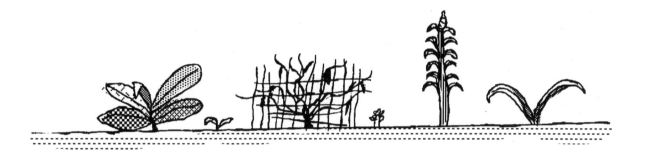

Two days later, I looked out the window with Rosie
and saw the rat.

Rosie's Rat came back!

ROSIE; I was sitting at the breakfast table.
Porter looked out in the courtyard
and in the very same spot as before—
There was the rat!
The rat came back!
We went outside and picked her up
and brought her inside.
We played with her.
We let her go outside and live under the shed.
She still lives under the shed.

PORTER: She lives under the shed,
but whenever she comes back to the house
to get food, she goes under the stove
into the drawer and tries to make a nest.
She has doggy bones
and little pieces of the mop in her nest.
She runs around the house.
She doesn't eat turkeys.

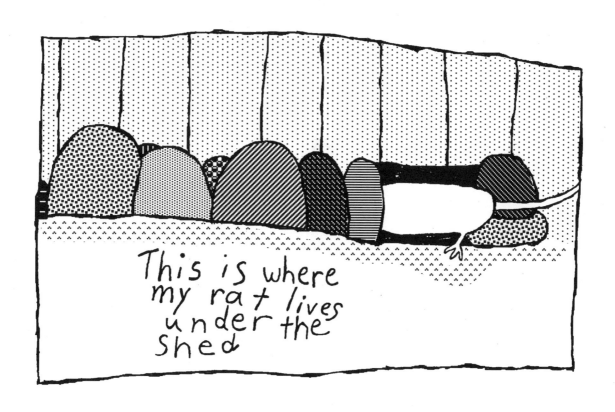

This is where
my rat lives
under the
shed

Me loving my rat.

ROSIE: I love my rat.

The End

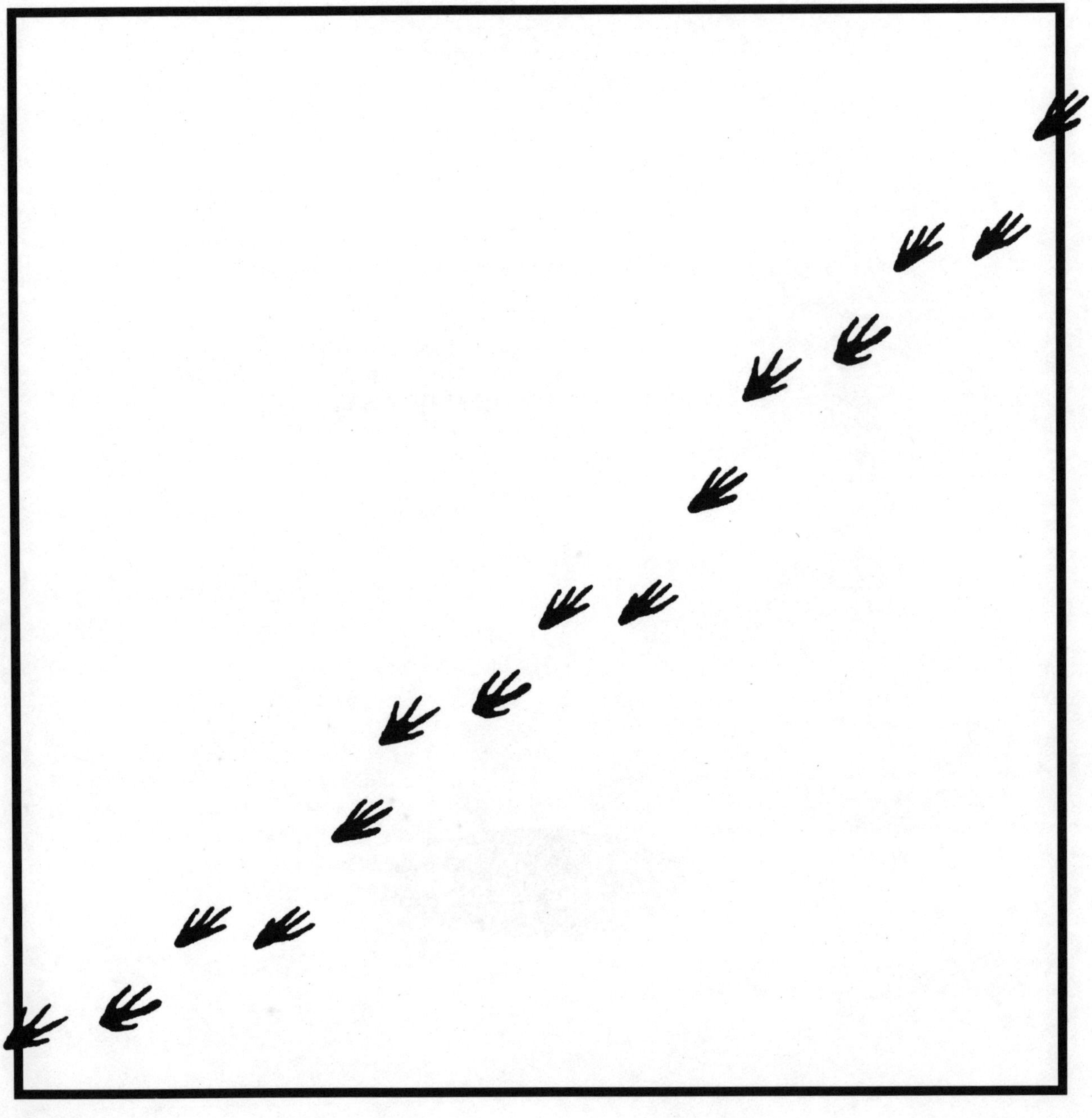

Porter Paul Swentzell
lives at Santa Clara Pueblo, New Mexico.
He has homeschooled for four years and hopes to keep homeschooling.
He likes making up games having to do with history,
also he enjoys being a Civil War re-enactor.
When he is in the right mood he writes on other stories.

Rose Swentzell
was born at the Santa Fe Indian Hospital in 1983.
She lives in Santa Clara Pueblo with her mother, stepdad (Joel),
and her brother (Porter). Rose likes animals, making things,
drawing and playing with her cousin and brother.
She homeschools. Her mom and stepdad teach her.

This book was set in **Gill Sans,** designed by Eric Gill in 1924.
Sturdy and finely proportioned... it always returns.
Titling and page numbers are in **Wild Thing,**
an "eyes&curlytail" typeface from David Rankowski.
Big Cheese— Bob & Eric & Emigre.

•

Book design by J. Bryan

Remember to say thank you.

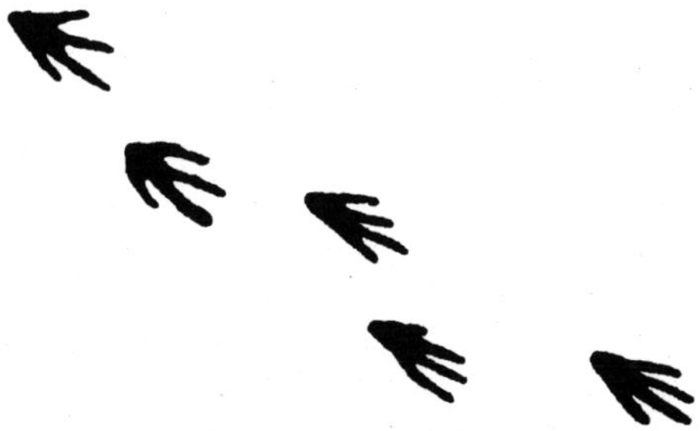